GREAT
CHILDREN'S
STORIES

The Classic Volland Edition

GREAT CHILDREN'S STORIES

The Classic Volland Edition

Illustrated by
FREDERICK RICHARDSON

CHECKERBOARD PRESS
NEW YORK

Because this book was planned
upon the knowledge of what children love
and of the changeless popularity of
the old, old stories it presents,
it is appreciatively dedicated to
all children

INTRODUCTION

by IRENE HUNT, *Author, Educator, Reading Consultant*
Newbery Award Winner

Here are the classic stories which for generations have constituted the heritage of children. Let no adult underestimate the delight they have afforded to the young throughout the decades. If you, as an adult, doubt that these stories have their place in the lives of modern children, take the time to seat yourself among a group of very young listeners and read the story of a patiently persistent Little Red Hen or a terrified Chicken Licken running in a frenzy from the falling sky. It will be a rewarding experience to find yourself the great giver of wonderful gifts.

The faces of children never fail to express the wonder and delight that the introduction to the world of literature brings to them. A new world is opened, a world that sings in the rhythmic sing-song of childhood, a world in which the ripples of imagination stretch far out to merge with the quiet waters of a deeper understanding of life.

This writer can dimly recall the age of three or four when someone told her for the first time the story of *The Three Bears.* I believed that the story was a gift made expressly for me, a thing of magic the like of which I had never dreamed. True, it made me greedy—for more—and from that hour the world of books, the joys of literature had a new disciple.

So it is with each succeeding generation. Children today have a more expansive environment—sometimes richer, but not always. They know more of the world about them, but they still respond to characters that charmed children years ago; not only very young children but older children whose lives have been left barren in an environment lacking books or story-telling.

At first glance, the sophisticated adult may question the word "magic" that is often applied to these stories. The conclusion may be that the stories are simple, repetitious, or unrealistic. But that conclusion needs to be examined.

First of all, the original authors or "tellers" or "singers" of these stories represent a small portion of adults—a most fortunate portion—whose early memories stayed with them, and whose closeness to the feelings, the needs, the bewilderment, delight and humor of childhood has never left them. Too many adults have forgotten the feeling of being a child, too many have felt (and still do) that writing a story for children must be as simple as writing a friendly letter. But not many stories written by such an adult will ever endure as these classic tales have.

On the other hand, a story such as "Charlotte's Web" seems likely to live indefinitely. I believe Maurice Sendak's *Where the Wild Things Are*

may achieve the same immortality; and I can't help but believe that A. A. Milne's *Winnie the Pooh* will live as long as the little pig who built the best house and out-maneuvered the wolf. But these are only a few, and they are the work of people who, like the authors of the Mother Goose stories, have somehow in the midst of the pressures of maturity, retained their understanding of what it is that penetrates and curls up cozily within a child's imagination.

Young readers and listeners are not squeamish. Children of decades long past as well as those today have casually accepted the lusty, gusty world of suspense and fright, of gobbling up (and being gobbled), of snooping and being very nearly done-in (as was Goldilocks), of outwitting evil (in the form of a bad fox) by quick thinking and considerable ingenuity. They remember the incidents that were spine tingling ("I'll huff and I'll puff and I'll blow your house in"); and the situations that were fraught with a satisfying sense of justice (The little red hen).

There is always in life, even in the lives of the very young, some situations of stress, some predicaments that lead to bewilderment and anxiety. The old stories mirror these predicaments, and the literature of adults develops from the basic anxieties and needs that have become more complex as life has progressed. Chicken Licken believes that the sky is falling and certainly such a possibility is horrifying. Falling is closely allied to pain from the child's earliest memories of learning to walk or of exploring heights too much for him. And so he can recognize Chicken Licken's frenzy of fear. And years later, there may appear a very faint memory of Chicken Licken, as the child, grown to adulthood, watches mad King Lear running in terror upon the moors!

In this book the art most delightfully adds a new dimension to the retelling of the stories. Each artist throughout the years has, by his own perception of characters and situations, given something new and original to the telling of the stories. In this book, Frederick Richardson supplies a wealth of detail in rich colors as well as a quiet humor which the child will happily discover. To see Goldilocks enter a proper and well-ordered house a little before eight o'clock and then, on the next page, to find the ways in which she has created havoc by a little after nine is a delight that will forever embellish the story of *The Three Bears* for the child. And come to think of it, who but Frederick Richardson has ever told us that the pig's reluctance to cross the stile had something to do with sight of whey dripping from a cheese bag. And what child will not chuckle when he sees the stiff-necked indifference of the duck, the cat and the dog when the little hen first finds the bag of wheat and, a few pages later, their eager interest when the loaf of bread is ready to eat.

And so here is a book full of many delights, old and new. I hope it reaches many children and that it makes them as happy as it does many of us who can still remember childhood.

CONTENTS

The LITTLE RED HEN

One day as the little Red Hen was scratching in a
field, she found a grain of wheat.

"This wheat should be planted," she said. "Who
will plant this grain of wheat?"

"Not I," said the Duck.

"Not I," said the Cat.

"Not I," said the Dog.

"Then I will," said Little Red Hen. And she did.

Soon the wheat grew to be tall and yellow.

"The wheat is ripe," said the Little Red Hen.

"Who will cut the wheat?"

"Not I," said the Duck.

"Not I," said the Cat.

"Not I," said the Dog.

"Then I will," said Little Red Hen. And she did.

When the wheat was cut, the Little Red Hen said,
"Who will thresh this wheat?"

"Not I," said the Duck.

"Not I," said the Cat.

"Not I," said the Dog.

"Then I will," said Little Red Hen. And she did.
When the wheat was all threshed, the Little Red
Hen said, "Who'll take this wheat to the mill?"

"Not I," said the Duck.

"Not I," said the Cat.

"Not I," said the Dog.

"Then I will," said the Little Red Hen. And she did.

She took the wheat to the mill and had it ground into flour. Then she said, "Who will make this flour into bread?"

"Not I," said the Duck.

"Not I," said the Cat.

"Not I," said the Dog.

"Then I will," said the Little Red Hen. And she did.

She made and baked the bread. Then she said, "Who will eat this bread?"

"Oh! I will," said the Duck.

"And I will," said the Cat.

"And I will," said the Dog.

"No, no!" said the Little Red Hen. "I will do that."
And she did.

THE TRAVELS
OF A FOX

Afox was digging behind a stump, and he found a
bumble-bee. The fox put the bumble-bee in a
bag and he traveled.

The first house he came to he went in, and he said
to the mistress of the house: "May I leave my bag

here while I go to Squintum's?"

"Yes," said the woman.

"Then be careful not to open the bag," said the fox.

As soon as the fox was out of sight, the woman took a little peep in the bag and out flew the bumble-bee, and the rooster caught him and ate him up.

After a while the fox came back. He took up his bag and he saw that his bumble-bee was gone, and he said to the woman: "Where is my bumble-bee?"

And the woman said: "I just untied the bag, and then the bumble-bee flew out, and the rooster ate him up."

"Very well," said the fox, "I must have the rooster, then."

So he caught the rooster and put him in his bag,
and traveled.

And the next house he came to he went in, and
said to the mistress of the house: "May I leave my bag
here while I go to Squintum's?"

"Yes, said the woman.

"Then be careful not to open the bag," said the fox.

But as soon as the fox was out of sight, the woman just took a little peep into the bag, and the rooster flew out, and the pig caught him and ate him up.

After a while the fox came back, and he took up his bag and he saw that the rooster was not in it, and he said to the woman: "Where is my rooster?"

And the woman said: "I just untied the bag, and the rooster flew out, and the pig ate him."

"Very well," said the fox, "I must have the pig, then."

So he caught the pig and put him in his bag, and traveled.

And the next house he came to he went in, and said to the mistress of the house: "May I leave my bag here while I go to Squintum's?"

"Yes," said the woman.

"Then be careful not to open the bag," said the fox.

But as soon as the fox was out of sight, the woman just took a little peep into the bag, and the pig jumped out, and the ox ate him.

After a while the fox came back. He took up his bag and he saw that the pig was gone, and he said to the woman: "Where is my pig?"

And the woman said: "I just untied the bag, and the pig jumped out, and the ox ate him."

"Very well," said the fox, "I must have the ox."

So he caught the ox and put him in his bag, and traveled.

And the next house he came to he went in, and said to the mistress of the house: "May I leave my bag here while I go to Squintum's?"

"Yes," said the woman.

"Then be careful not to open the bag," said the fox.

But as soon as the fox was out of sight, the woman just took a little peep in the bag, and the ox got out, and the woman's little boy chased him away off over the fields.

After a while the fox came back. He took up his bag and he saw that his ox was gone, and he said to the woman: "Where is my ox?"

And the woman said: "I just untied the string, and the ox got out, and my little boy chased him away off over the fields."

"Very well," said the fox, "I must have the little boy, then."

So he caught the little boy and put him in his bag, and traveled.

And the next house he came to he went in, and

said to the mistress of the house: "May I leave my bag here while I go to Squintum's?"

"Yes," said the woman.

"Then be careful not to open the bag," said the fox.

The woman was making cake, and her children were around her asking for some.

"Oh, mother, give me a piece," said one; and, "Oh, mother, give me a piece," said the others.

And the smell of the cake came to the little boy who was weeping and crying in the bag, and he heard the children asking for cake and he said: "Oh, mother, give me a piece."

Then the woman opened the bag and took the little boy out, and she put the house-dog in the bag in the little boy's place.

And the little boy stopped crying and had some cake with the others.

After a while the fox came back. He took up his bag and he saw that it was tied fast, and he put it over

his back and traveled far into the deep woods. Then he sat down and untied the bag, and if the little boy had been there in the bag things would have gone badly with him.

But the little boy was safe at the woman's house, and when the fox untied the bag the house-dog jumped out and ate him all up.

The THREE BEARS

In a far-off country, once upon a time, there was a little girl who was called Goldilocks because of her beautiful golden curls.

Goldilocks loved to romp and play. She loved to run into the woods to gather wild flowers, or to chase

butterflies through the open fields.

One day she ran here and she ran there, until at
last she found herself in a strange and lonely wood. In
the wood she saw a snug little house in which three
bears lived. But Goldilocks did not know that three

bears lived in this house. One was a Great Big Bear, and one was a Middle-sized bear, and one was a Wee Little Bear.

The door of the little house was open; so Goldilocks peeped in and saw that it was quite empty. She stepped inside to look about a bit; no one was home. The three bears had just gone out for a walk. They had left their three bowls of porridge on the table to cool.

The porridge smelled very good, and Goldilocks thought that she would like to taste it. So she tasted the porridge in the great big bowl, which belonged to the Great Big Bear, but she found it too hot.

Then she tasted the porridge in the middle-sized bowl, which belonged to the Middle-sized Bear, but she found it too cold.

Then she tasted the porridge in the wee little bowl, which belonged to the Wee Little Bear. This porridge was just right, and she ate it all.

Goldilocks then looked about the room and saw three chairs. She thought she would try the great big chair, which belonged to the Great Big Bear, but she

found it too hard.

She then tried the middle-sized chair, which belonged to the Middle-sized Bear, but she found it too soft.

So she tried the wee little chair, which belonged to

the Wee Little Bear, and she found it just right. But when she sat in the wee little chair, she broke it.

By this time Goldilocks was very tired, and she went into another room where she saw three beds. She tried the great big bed, which belonged to the Great Big Bear, but she found it too high at the head for her.

Then she tried the middle-sized bed, which belonged to the Middle-sized Bear, but she found it too high at the foot for her.

She then tried the wee little bed, which belonged to the Wee Little Bear, and she found it just right; so she lay down upon it and fell fast asleep.

While Goldilocks was lying fast asleep, the three

bears came home from their walk, and they went quickly to the kitchen to get their porridge.

The Great Big Bear looked into his bowl and said in his great big voice, "Somebody has been tasting my porridge!"

Then the Middle-sized Bear looked into her bowl and said in her middle-sized voice, "Somebody has been tasting my porridge!"

And the Wee Little Bear looked into his bowl and cried in his wee little voice, "Somebody has been

tasting my porridge, and has eaten it all up!"

Then they looked at their chairs and the Great Big Bear said, "Somebody has been sitting in my chair!"

And the Middle-sized Bear said, "Somebody has been sitting in my chair!"

And the Wee Little Bear cried, "Somebody has been sitting in my chair and has broken it all to pieces!"

The three bears then went into their bedroom, and the Great Big Bear said, "Somebody has been lying in my bed!"

And the Middle-sized Bear said, "Somebody has been lying in my bed!"

And the Wee Little Bear cried, "Somebody has been lying in my bed, and here she is!"

At that, Goldilocks woke in a fright and jumped out of the nearest window. She ran away as fast as her legs could carry her, and she never went again to the snug little house of the Three Bears.

THE STRAW OX

There was once upon a time an old man and an old woman. The old man worked in the fields as a pitch burner, while the old woman sat at home and spun flax. They were so poor that they could save nothing at all; all their earnings went in bare food, and when that was gone there was nothing left. At last the old woman had a good idea.

"Look, now, husband," cried she, "make me a straw ox, and smear it all over with tar."

"Why, you foolish woman!" said he, "what's the good of such an ox?"

"Never mind," said she, "you just make it. I know what I am about."

What was the poor man to do?

He set to work and made the ox of straw, and smeared it all over with tar.

The night passed away, and at early dawn the old woman took her distaff and drove the straw ox out to graze, and she herself sat down behind a hillock and began spinning her flax, and cried:

"Graze away, little ox, while I spin my flax; graze away, little ox, while I spin my flax!" And while she spun, her head drooped down, and she began to doze, and while she was dozing, from behind the dark wood and from the back of the huge pines a bear came rushing out upon the ox and said:

"Who are you? Speak and tell me!"

And the ox said:

"A three-year-old heifer am I, made of straw and smeared with tar."

"Oh!" said the bear, "stuffed with straw and trimmed with tar, are you? Then give me of your straw and tar, that I may patch up my ragged fur!"

"Take some," said the ox, and the bear fell upon him and began to tear away at the tar.

He tore and tore, and buried his teeth in it till he found he couldn't let go again. He tugged and he tugged, but it was no good, and the ox dragged him gradually off, goodness knows where.

Then the old woman awoke, and there was no ox to be seen. "Alas! old fool that I am!" cried she, "perchance it has gone home."

Then she quickly caught up her distaff and spinning-board, threw them over her shoulders, and hastened off home, and she saw that the ox had dragged the bear up to the fence, and in she went to her old man. "Dad, dad!" she cried, "look, look! The ox has brought us a bear. Come out and kill it!"

Then the old man jumped up, tore off the bear,

tied him up, and threw him in the cellar.

Next morning, between dark and dawn, the old woman took her distaff and drove the ox into the steppe to graze. She herself sat down by a mound, began spinning, and said:

"Graze, graze away, little ox, while I spin my flax!
graze, graze away, little ox, while I spin my flax!"
And while she spun, her head drooped down, and she
dozed. And, lo! from behind the dark wood, from the
back of the huge pines, a gray wolf came rushing out

upon the ox and said:

"Who are you? Come, tell me!"

"I am a three-year-old heifer, stuffed with straw and trimmed with tar," said the ox.

"Oh, trimmed with tar, are you? Then give me of your tar to tar my sides, that the dogs and the sons of dogs tear me not!"

"Take some," said the ox. And with that the wolf fell upon him and tried to tear the tar off. He tugged and tugged and tore with his teeth, but could get none off. Then he tried to let go, and couldn't; tug and worry as he might, it was no good.

When the old woman woke, there was no ox in sight. "Maybe my ox has gone home!" she cried; "I'll go home and see."

When she got there she was astonished, for by the paling stood the ox with the wolf still tugging at it. She ran and told her old man, and her old man came and threw the wolf into the cellar also.

On the third day the woman again drove her ox into the pastures to graze, and sat down by a mound and dozed off.

Then a fox came running up. "Who are you?" it asked the ox.

"I'm a three-year-old heifer, stuffed with straw and daubed with tar."

"Then give me some of your tar to smear my sides, when those dogs and sons of dogs tear my hide!"

"Take some," said the ox. Then the fox fastened her teeth in him and couldn't draw them out again. The old woman told her old man, and he took and cast the fox into the cellar in the same way. And after that they caught Pussy Swiftfoot likewise.

So when he had got them all safely, the old man sat down on a bench before the cellar and began sharpening a knife. And the bear said to him:

"Tell me, daddy, what are you sharpening your knife for?"

"To flay your skin off, that I may make a leather jacket for myself and a pelisse for my old woman."

"Oh, don't flay me, daddy dear! Rather let me go, and I'll bring you a lot of honey."

"Very well, see that you do it," and he unbound and let the bear go. Then he sat down on the bench

and again began sharpening his knife. And the wolf
asked him:

"Daddy, what are you sharpening your knife for?"

"To flay off your skin, that I may make me a warm
cap against the winter."

"Oh! Don't flay me, daddy dear, and I'll bring you a whole herd of little sheep."

"Well, see that you do it," and he let the wolf go.

Then he sat down, and began sharpening his knife again.

The fox put out her little snout, and asked him:

"Be so kind, dear daddy, and tell me why you are sharpening your knife?"

"Little foxes," said the old man, "have nice skins that do capitally for collars and trimmings, and I want to skin you!"

"Oh! Don't take my skin away, daddy dear, and I will bring you hens and geese."

"Very well, see that you do it!" and he let the fox go.

The hare now alone remained and the old man began sharpening his knife on the hare's account.

"Why do you do that?" asked puss, and he replied:

"Little hares have nice little, soft, warm skins, which will make me nice gloves and mittens against the winter!"

"Oh, daddy dear! Don't flay me, and I'll bring you kale and good cauliflower, if only you let me go!"

Then he let the hare go also.

They then went to bed, but very early in the morning, when it was neither dusk nor dawn, there

was a noise in the doorway like "Durrrrrr!"

"Daddy!" cried the old woman, "there's some one scratching at the door; go and see who it is!"

The old man went out, and there was the bear carrying a whole hive full of honey. The old man took the honey from the bear.

No sooner did he lie down than again there was another "Durrrrr!" at the door. The old man looked out and saw the wolf driving a whole flock of sheep into the courtyard. Close on his heels came the fox,

46

driving before him geese and hens, and all manner of fowls; and last of all came the hare, bringing cabbage and kale, and all manner of good food.

And the old man was glad, and the old woman was glad. And the old man sold the sheep and oxen, and got so rich that he needed nothing more.

As for the straw-stuffed ox, it stood in the sun till it fell to pieces.

The OLD WOMAN AND HER PIG

An old woman found a crooked sixpence while sweeping her door-yard. "What shall I do with this sixpence?" she said. "I will go to the market and buy a pig."

Then the old woman went to the market and

bought a pig. On her way home she came to a stile and then the pig would not go over the stile.

"Pig, pig, get over the stile,
    Or I can not get home tonight."
But the pig would not.

Then she went a little farther and met a dog; and she said to the dog:

"Dog, dog, bite pig;
    Pig won't get over the stile;
    And I can not get home tonight."
But the dog would not.

Then she went a little farther and met a stick; and she said to the stick:

"Stick, stick, beat the dog;
    Dog won't bite pig;
    Pig won't get over the stile;
    And I can not get home tonight."
But the stick would not.

Then she went a little farther and met a fire; and she said to the fire:

"Fire, fire, burn stick;

Stick won't beat dog;

Dog won't bite pig;

Pig won't get over the stile;

And I can not get home tonight."

But the fire would not.

Then she went a little farther and met some water;
and she said to the water:

"Water, water, quench fire;

Fire won't burn stick;

Stick won't beat dog;

Dog won't bite pig;

Pig won't get over the stile;

And I can not get home tonight."

But the water would not.

Then she went a little farther and met an ox; and

she said to the ox:

> "Ox, ox, drink water;
>
> Water won't quench fire;
>
> Fire won't burn stick;
>
> Stick won't beat dog;
>
> Dog won't bite pig;
>
> Pig won't get over the stile;
>
> And I can not get home tonight."

But the ox would not.

Then she went a little farther and met a butcher; and she said to the butcher:

> "Butcher, butcher, pen ox;
>
> Ox won't drink water;
>
> Water won't quench fire;
>
> Fire won't burn stick;
>
> Stick won't beat dog;
>
> Dog won't bite pig;
>
> Pig won't get over the stile;
>
> And I can not get home tonight."

But the butcher would not.

Then she went a little farther and met a rope; and she said to the rope:

"Rope, rope, whip butcher;
Butcher, won't pen ox;
Ox won't drink water;
Water won't quench fire;
Fire won't burn stick;

Stick won't beat dog;

Dog won't bite pig;

Pig won't get over the stile;

And I can not get home tonight."

But the rope would not.

Then she went a little farther and met a rat; and she said to the rat:

"Rat, rat, gnaw rope;

Rope won't whip butcher;

Butcher won't pen ox;

Ox won't drink water;

Water won't quench fire;

Fire won't burn stick;

Stick won't beat dog;

Dog won't bite pig;

Pig won't get over the stile;

And I can not get home tonight."

But the rat would not.

Then she went a little farther and met a cat; and she said to the cat:

"Cat, cat, bite rat;

Rat won't gnaw rope;

Rope won't whip butcher;
Butcher won't pen ox;
Ox won't drink water;
Water won't quench fire;
Fire won't burn stick;

Stick won't beat dog;

Dog won't bite pig;

Pig won't get over the stile;

And I can not get home tonight."

But the cat said to her, "If you will get me a saucer

of milk, I will bite the rat." Then the old woman gave a wisp of hay to a cow that was near, and the cow gave her a saucer of milk. Then the old woman gave the saucer of milk to the cat and this is what happened:

The cat began to bite the rat; the rat began to gnaw the rope; the rope began to whip the butcher; the butcher began to pen the ox; the ox began to drink the water; the water began to quench the fire; the fire began to burn the stick; the stick began to beat the dog; the dog began to bite the pig; the pig got over the stile; and the old woman got home that night.

The THREE LITTLE PIGS

Long ago there lived a pig who had three little pigs.
The mother pig was very poor, and at last she
had to send her little pigs out to seek their fortunes.

The first little pig that went away met a man with a
bundle of straw, and he said to him, "Please, man,

give me that straw to build me a house."

The man gave the straw to the little pig. Then the pig built a house of the straw, and lived in the house.

By and by a wolf came along and knocked at the door of the little straw house.

"Little pig, little pig, let me come in!" called the wolf.

"No, no, by the hair of my chinny, chin, chin, I'll not let you in," answered the pig.

"Then I'll huff and I'll puff and I'll blow your

house in," said the wolf.

So he huffed and he puffed and he blew the house in. Then he chased the little pig away.

The second little pig that went away met a man with a bundle of sticks, and he said to the man, "Please, man, give me your bundle of sticks to build me a house."

The man gave the sticks to the little pig. Then the pig built a house of the sticks, and lived in the house.

By and by the wolf came along and knocked at the door of the little house of sticks.

"Little pig, little pig, let me come in!" called the wolf.

"No, no, by the hair of my chinny, chin, chin, I'll not let you in," answered the pig.

"Then I'll huff and I'll puff and I'll blow your house in," said the wolf.

So he huffed and he puffed and he blew the house in. Then he chased the little pig away.

The third little pig that went away met a man with a load of bricks, and he said, "Please, man, give me your load of bricks to build me a house."

The man gave the bricks to the little pig. Then the
pig built a house with the bricks and lived in the
house.

At last the wolf came along and knocked at the
door of the brick house.

"Little pig, little pig, let me come in!" called the wolf.

"No, no, by the hair of my chinny, chin, chin, I'll not let you in," answered the pig.

"Then I'll huff and I'll puff and I'll blow your

house in," said the wolf.

So he huffed and he puffed and he puffed and he huffed, but he could not blow the little brick house in.

The wolf rested a few minutes, and then he said, "Little pig, little pig, will you let just the tip of my nose in?"

"No," said the little pig.

"Little pig, little pig, will you let just my paw in?"

"No," said the little pig.

"Little pig, little pig, will you let just the tip of my tail in?"

"No," said the little pig.

"Then I will climb up on the roof and come down through the chimney," said the wolf.

But the little pig made the fire very hot, so the wolf could not come down the chimney. So he went away, and that was the end of him.

The little pig then went and fetched his mother, and they still live happily in their little brick house.

TITTY MOUSE and TATTY MOUSE

Titty Mouse and Tatty Mouse both lived in a house.

Titty Mouse went a-leasing, to gather up the fallen ears of corn, and Tatty Mouse went a-leasing.

So they both went a-leasing.

Titty Mouse leased an ear of corn, and Tatty Mouse leased an ear of corn.

So they both leased an ear of corn.

Titty Mouse made a pudding, and Tatty Mouse made a pudding.

So they both made a pudding.

And Tatty Mouse put her pudding into the pot to boil.

But when Titty went to put hers in, the pot tumbled over and scalded her to death.

Then Tatty sat down and wept; then a three-legged stool said:

"Tatty, why do you weep?"

"Titty's dead," said Tatty, "and so I weep."

"Then," said the stool, "I'll hop," so the stool

hopped. Then a broom in the corner of the room said: "Stool, why do you hop?" "Oh!" said the stool, "Titty's dead, and Tatty weeps, and so I hop." "Then," said the broom, "I'll sweep," so the broom began to sweep.

"Then," said the door, "Broom, why do you sweep?" "Oh!" said the broom, "Titty's dead, and Tatty weeps, and the stool hops, and so I sweep." "Then," said the door, "I'll jar," so the door jarred.

"Then," said the window, "Door, why do you jar?" "Oh!" said the door, "Titty's dead, and Tatty weeps, and the stool hops, and the broom sweeps, and so I jar."

"Then," said the window, "I'll creak," so the window creaked.

Now there was an old bench outside the house, and when the window creaked, the bench said: "Window, why do you creak?" "Oh!" said the window, "Titty's dead, and Tatty weeps, and the stool hops, the broom sweeps, the door jars, and so I creak."

"Then," said the bench, "I'll run round the house." Then the old bench ran round the house.

Now there was a fine large walnut-tree growing by the cottage, and the tree said to the bench: "Bench, why do you run round the house?" "Oh!" said the bench, "Titty's dead, and Tatty weeps, and the stool

hops, and the broom sweeps, the door jars, and the window creaks, and so I run round the house."

"Then," said the walnut-tree, "I'll shed my leaves."

So the walnut-tree shed all its beautiful green leaves.

Now there was a little bird perched on one of the boughs of the tree, and when all the leaves fell, it said: "Walnut-tree, why do you shed your leaves?" "Oh!" said the tree, "Titty's dead, and Tatty weeps, the stool hops, and the broom sweeps, the door jars, and the window creaks, the old bench runs round the house, and so I shed my leaves."

"Then," said the little bird, "I'll moult all my feathers," so he moulted all his pretty feathers. Now there was a little girl walking below, carrying a jug of milk for her brothers' and sisters' supper, and when she saw the poor little bird moult all its feathers, she said: "Little bird, why do you moult all your feathers?" "Oh!" said the little bird, "Titty's dead, and Tatty weeps, and the stool hops, and the broom sweeps, and the door jars, and the window creaks, and the old bench runs round the house, the walnut-tree sheds its leaves, and so I moult all my feathers."

"Then," said the little girl, "I'll spill the milk," so she dropt the pitcher and spilt the milk.

Now there was an old man just by on the top of a ladder thatching a rick, and when he saw the little girl spill the milk, he said: "Little girl, what do you mean by spilling the milk? Your little brothers and sisters must go without their supper."

Then said the little girl: "Titty's dead, and Tatty weeps, and the stool hops, and the broom sweeps, the door jars, and the window creaks, the old bench runs round the house, the walnut-tree sheds all its leaves, the little bird moults all its feathers, and so I spill the milk."

"Oh!" said the old man, "then I'll tumble off the ladder and break my neck," so he tumbled off the ladder and broke his neck.

When the old man broke his neck, the great walnut-tree fell down with a crash, and upset the old bench and house, and the house falling knocked the window out, and the window knocked the door down, and the door upset the broom, and the broom upset the stool, and poor little Tatty Mouse was buried beneath the ruins.

JOHNNY and the THREE GOATS

Every morning Johnny drove his three goats to pasture and every evening when the sun was going to bed he brought them home.

One morning he set off early, driving the goats before him and whistling as he trudged along.

Just as he reached Mr. Smith's turnip field what should he see but a broken board in the fence.

The goats saw it too, and in they skipped and began running round and round, stopping now and then to nip off the tops of the tender young turnips.

Johnny knew that would never do.

Picking up a stick he climbed through the fence and tried to drive the goats out.

But never were there such provoking goats.

Round and round they went, not once looking toward the hole in the fence.

Johnny ran and ran and ran till he could run no farther, and then he crawled through the hole in the fence and sat down beside the road and began to cry.

Just then who should come down the road but the fox.

"Good morning, Johnny!" said he. "What are you crying about?"

"I'm crying because I can't get the goats out of the turnip field," said Johnny.

"Oh, don't cry about that," said the fox. "I'll drive them out for you."

So over the fence leaped the fox, and round and round the turnip field he ran after the goats.

But no, they would not go out.

They flicked their tails and shook their heads and away they went, trampling down the turnips until you could hardly have told what had been growing in the field.

The fox ran till he could run no more.

Then he went over and sat down beside Johnny, and he began to cry.

Down the road came a rabbit.

"Good morning, Fox," said he. "What are you crying about?"

"I'm crying because Johnny is crying," said the fox, "and Johnny is crying because he can't get the goats out of the turnip field."

"Tut, tut!" said the rabbit, "what a thing to cry about! Watch me. I'll soon drive them out."

The rabbit hopped over the fence.

Round and round the field he chased the goats; but they would not go near the hole in the fence.

At last the rabbit was so tired he could not hop another hop.

He too crawled through the fence, sat down beside the fox, and began to cry.

Just then a bee came buzzing along over the tops of the flowers.

When she saw the rabbit she said, "Good morning, Bunny, what are you crying about?"

"I'm crying because the fox is crying," said the rabbit, "and the fox is crying because Johnny is crying, and Johnny is crying because he can't get the goats out of the turnip field."

"Don't cry about that," said the bee, "I'll soon get them out for you."

"You!" said the rabbit, "a little thing like you drive the goats out, when neither Johnny, nor the fox, nor I can get them out?" and he laughed at the very idea of such a thing.

"Watch me," said the bee.

Over the fence she flew and buzz-z-z she went

right in the ear of the biggest goat.

The goat shook his head and tried to brush away the bee, but the bee only flew to the other ear and buzz-z-z she went, until the goat thought there must be some dreadful thing in the turnip field, so out through the hole in the fence he went, and ran down the road to his pasture.

The bee flew over to the second goat and buzz-z-z she went first in one ear and then in the other, until that goat was willing to follow the other through the fence and down the road to the pasture.

The bee flew after the third goat and buzzed first in one ear and then in the other until he too was glad to follow the others.

"Thank you, little bee," said Johnny and wiping away his tears, he hurried down the road to put the goats in the pasture.

CHICKEN LICKEN

One day when Chicken Licken was scratching among the leaves, an acorn fell out of a tree and struck her on the tail.

"Oh," said Chicken Licken, "the sky is falling! I am going to tell the King."

So she went along and went along until she met Henny Penny.

"Good morning, Chicken Licken, where are you going?" said Henny Penny.

"Oh, Henny Penny, the sky is falling and I am going to tell the King!"

"How do you know the sky is falling?" asked Henny Penny.

"I saw it with my own eyes, I heard it with my own ears, and a piece of it fell on my tail!" said Chicken Licken.

"Then I will go with you," said Henny Penny.

So they went along and went along until they met Cocky Locky.

"Good morning, Henny Penny and Chicken Licken," said Cocky Locky, "where are you going?"

"Oh, Cocky Locky, the sky is falling, and we are going to tell the King!"

"How do you know the sky is falling?" asked Cocky Locky.

"Chicken Licken told me," said Henny Penny.

"I saw it with my own eyes, I heard it with my

own ears, and a piece of it fell on my tail!" said
Chicken Licken.

"Then I will go with you," said Cocky Locky, "and
we will tell the King."

So they went along and went along until they met

Ducky Daddles.

"Good morning, Cocky Locky, Henny Penny, and Chicken Licken," said Ducky Daddles, "where are you going?"

"Oh, Ducky Daddles, the sky is falling and we are

going to tell the King!"

"How do you know the sky is falling?" asked Ducky Daddles.

"Henny Penny told me," said Cocky Locky.

"Chicken Licken told me," said Henny Penny.

"I saw it with my own eyes, I heard it with my own ears, and a piece of it fell on my tail!" said Chicken Licken.

"Then I will go with you," said Ducky Daddles, "and we will tell the King."

So they went along and went along until they met Goosey Loosey.

"Good morning, Ducky Daddles, Cocky Locky, Henny Penny, and Chicken Licken," said Goosey Loosey, "where are you going?"

"Oh, Goosey Loosey, the sky is falling and we are going to tell the King!"

"How do you know the sky is falling?" asked Goosey Loosey.

"Cocky Locky told me," said Ducky Daddles.

"Henny Penny told me," said Cocky Locky.

"Chicken Licken told me," said Henny Penny.

"I saw it with my own eyes, I heard it with my own ears, and a piece of it fell on my tail!" said Chicken Licken.

"Then I will go with you," said Goosey Loosey, "and we will tell the King!"

So they went along and went along until they met Turkey Lurkey.

"Good morning, Goosey Loosey, Ducky Daddles, Cocky Locky, Henny Penny, and Chicken Licken," said Turkey Lurkey, "where are you going?"

"Oh, Turkey Lurkey, the sky is falling and we are going to tell the King!"

"How do you know the sky is falling?" asked Turkey Lurkey.

"Ducky Daddles told me," said Goosey Loosey.

"Cocky Locky told me," said Ducky Daddles.

"Henny Penny told me," said Cocky Locky.

"Chicken Licken told me," said Henny Penny.

"I saw it with my own eyes, I heard it with my own ears, and a piece of it fell on my tail!" said Chicken Licken.

"Then I will go with you," said Turkey Lurkey,

"and we will tell the King!"

So they went along and went along until they met Foxy Woxy.

"Good morning, Turkey Lurkey, Goosey Loosey, Ducky Daddles, Cocky Locky, Henny Penny, and

Chicken Licken," said Foxy Woxy, "where are you going?"

"Oh, Foxy Woxy, the sky is falling and we are going to tell the King!"

"How do you know the sky is falling?" asked

Foxy Woxy.

"Goosey Loosey told me," said Turkey Lurkey.

"Ducky Daddles told me," said Goosey Loosey.

"Cocky Locky told me," said Ducky Daddles.

"Henny Penny told me," said Cocky Locky.

"Chicken Licken told me," said Henny Penny.

"I saw it with my own eyes, I heard it with my own ears, and a piece of it fell on my tail," said Chicken Licken.

"Then we will run, we will run to my den," said Foxy Woxy, "and I will tell the King."

So they all ran to Foxy Woxy's den, and the King was never told that the sky was falling.

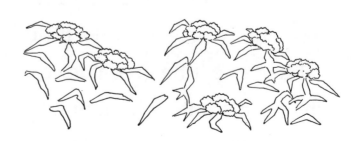

The COCK ~ The MOUSE and the LITTLE RED HEN

Once upon a time there was a hill, and on the hill there was a pretty little house.

It had one little green door, and four little windows with green shutters, and in it there lived a Cock, and a Mouse, and a Little Red Hen.

Close by was another little house. It was very ugly; had a door that wouldn't shut, and two broken windows, and all the paint was off its shutters. And in this house there lived a Bold Bad Fox and Four Bad Little Foxes.

One morning these four bad little foxes came to the big bad Fox, and said: "Oh, Father, we're so hungry!"

"We had nothing to eat yesterday," said one.

"And scarcely anything the day before," said another.

"And only half a chicken the day before that," said the third.

"And only two little ducks the day before that," said the fourth.

The bad Fox shook his head for a time, for he was thinking. At last he said in a big gruff voice:

"On the hill over there I see a house. And in that house there lives a Cock."

"And a Mouse," screamed two of the little foxes.

"And a little Red Hen," screamed the other two.

"And they are nice and fat," went on the big bad

Fox. "This very day, I'll take my great sack, and I will go up that hill, and in at that door, and into my sack I will put the Cock, and the Mouse, and the little Red Hen.

"I'll make a fire to roast the Cock," said one little fox.

"I'll put on the sauce-pan to boil the hen," said the second.

"And I'll get the frying pan to fry the mouse," said the third.

"And I'll have the biggest helping when they are all cooked," said the fourth, who was the greediest of all.

So the four little foxes jumped for joy, and the big bad Fox went to get his sack ready to start upon his journey.

But what was happening to the Cock and the Mouse, and the little Red Hen, all this time?

Well, sad to say, the Cock and the Mouse had both got out of bed on the wrong side that morning. The Cock said the day was too hot, and the Mouse grumbled because it was too cold.

They came grumbling down to the kitchen, where
the good little Red Hen, looking as bright as a
sunbeam, was bustling about.

"Who'll get some sticks to light the fire with?" she
asked.

"I shan't," said the Cock.

"I shan't," said the Mouse.

"Then I'll do it myself," said the little Red Hen.

So off she ran to get the sticks.

"And now, who'll fill the kettle from the spring?" she asked.

"I shan't," said the Cock.

"I shan't," said the Mouse.

"Then I'll do it myself," said the little Red Hen.

And off she ran to fill the kettle.

"And who'll get the breakfast ready?" she asked, as she put the kettle on to boil.

"I shan't," said the Cock.

"I shan't," said the Mouse.

"I'll do it myself," said the little Red Hen.

All breakfast time the Cock and the Mouse quarreled and grumbled. The Cock upset the milk jug, and the Mouse scattered crumbs upon the floor.

"Who'll clear away the breakfast?" asked the poor little Red Hen, hoping they would soon leave off being cross.

"I shan't," said the Cock.

"I shan't," said the Mouse.

"Then I'll do it myself," said the little Red Hen.

So she cleared everything away, swept up the crumbs and brushed up the fire-place.

"And now, who'll help me to make the beds?"

"I shan't," said the Cock.

"I shan't," said the Mouse.

"Then I'll do it myself," said the little Red Hen.

And she tripped away upstairs.

But the lazy Cock and Mouse each sat down in a comfortable arm-chair by the fire, and soon fell fast asleep.

Now the bad Fox had crept up the hill, and into the garden, and if the Cock and Mouse hadn't been asleep, they would have seen his sharp eyes peeping in at the window. "Rat tat tat, Rat tat tat," the Fox knocked at the door.

"Who can that be?" said the Mouse, half opening his eyes.

"Go and look for yourself, if you want to know," said the rude Cock.

"It's the postman perhaps," thought the Mouse to

himself, "and he may have a letter for me." So
without waiting to see who it was, he lifted the latch
and opened the door.

As soon as he opened it, in jumped the big Fox,
with a cruel smile upon his face!

"Oh! Oh! Oh!" squeaked the Mouse, as he tried to run up the chimney.

"Doodle doodle do!" screamed the Cock, as he jumped on the back of the biggest arm-chair.

But the Fox only laughed, and without more ado he took the little Mouse by the tail, and popped him into the sack, and seized the Cock by the neck and popped him in too.

Then the poor little Red Hen came running down-stairs to see what all the noise was about, and the Fox caught her and put her into the sack with the others. Then he took a long piece of string out of his pocket, wound it round and round and round the mouth of the sack, and tied it very tight indeed. After that he threw the sack over his back, and off he set down the hill.

"Oh! I wish I hadn't been so cross," said the Cock, as they went bumping about.

"Oh! I wish I hadn't been so lazy," said the Mouse, wiping his eyes with the tip of his tail.

"It's never too late to mend," said the little Red Hen.

"And don't be too sad. See, here I have my little work-bag, and in it there is a pair of scissors, and a little thimble, and a needle and thread. Very soon you will see what I am going to do."

Now the sun was very hot, and soon Mr. Fox began to feel his sack was heavy, and at last he thought he would lie down under a tree and go to sleep for a little while. So he threw the sack down with a big bump, and very soon fell fast asleep.

Snore, snore, snore, went the Fox.

As soon as the little Red Hen heard this, she took out her scissors, and began to snip a hole in the sack, just large enough for the Mouse to creep through.

"Quick," she whispered, "run as fast as you can and bring back a stone just as large as yourself."

Out scampered the Mouse, and soon came back, dragging a stone after him.

"Push it in here," said the little Red Hen, and he pushed it in in a twinkling.

Then the little Red Hen snipped away at the hole.

Soon it was large enough for the Cock to get through.

"Quick," she said, "run and get a stone as big as yourself."

Out flew the Cock, and soon came back quite out of breath with a big stone, which he pushed into the sack too.

Then the little Red Hen popped out, got a stone as big as herself, and pushed it in. Next she put on her thimble, took out her needle and thread, and sewed up the hole as quickly as ever she could.

When it was done, the Cock and the Mouse and the little Red Hen ran home very fast, shut the door after them, drew the bolts, shut the shutters, and drew down the blinds and felt quite safe.

The bad Fox lay fast asleep under the tree for some time, but at last he woke up.

"Dear, dear," he said, rubbing his eyes and then looking at the long shadows on the grass, "how late it is getting. I must hurry home."

So the bad Fox went grumbling and groaning down the hill, till he came to the stream.

Splash! In went one foot. Splash! In went the other, but the stones in the sack were so heavy that at the very next step down tumbled Mr. Fox into a deep pool.

And then the fishes carried him off to their fairy caves and kept him a prisoner there, so he was never seen again. And the four greedy little foxes had to go to bed without any supper.

But the Cock and the Mouse never grumbled again. They lit the fire, filled the kettle, laid the breakfast, and did all the work, while the good little Red Hen had a holiday, and sat resting in the big arm-chair.

No foxes ever troubled them again, and for all I know they are still living happily in the little house with the green door and green shutters, which stands on the hill.

THE BREMEN TOWN
MUSICIANS

There was a man who owned a donkey, which had carried his sacks to the mill industriously for many years, but whose strength had come to an end, so that the poor beast grew more and more unfit for work.

The master determined to stop his food.

But the donkey, discovering that there was no good intended to him, ran away and took the road to Bremen. "There," thought he, "I can turn Town Musician."

When he had gone a little way, he found a hound lying on the road and panting, like one who was tired with running.

"Hello! what are you panting so for, worthy seize 'em?" asked the donkey.

"Oh!" said the dog, "just because I am old, and get weaker every day, and cannot go out hunting, my master wanted to kill me, so I have taken leave of him; but how shall I gain my living now?"

"I'll tell you what," said the donkey. "I am going to Bremen to be Town Musician; come with me and take to music, too. I will play the lute, and you shall beat the drum."

The dog liked the idea, and they traveled on.

Soon they came upon a cat sitting by the road, making a face like three rainy days.

"Now then, what has gone wrong with you, old

Whiskers?'' said the donkey.

"Who can be merry when his neck is in danger?'' answered the cat. "Because I am advanced in years, and my teeth are blunt, and I like sitting before the fire and purring better than chasing the mice about, my mistress wanted to drown me. I have managed to escape. But good advice is scarce; tell me where I shall go to.''

"Come with us to Bremen. You understand serenading; you also can become a Town Musician.''

The cat thought it a capital idea, and went with them.

Soon after the three runaways came to a farmyard, and there sat a cock on the gate, crowing with might and main.

"You crow loud enough to deafen one," said the donkey. "What is the matter with you?"

"I prophesied fair weather," said the cock, "because it is our good mistress' washing day, and she wants to dry the clothes; but because tomorrow is Sunday, and company is coming, the mistress has no pity on me, and has told the cook to put me into the soup tomorrow, and I must have my head cut off to-night. So now I am crowing with all my might as long as I can."

"O you old Redhead," said the donkey, "you had better come with us; we are going to Bremen, where you will certainly find something better than having

your head cut off. You have a good voice, and if we all make music together, it will be something striking."

The cock liked the proposal, and they went on, all four together.

But they could not reach the city of Bremen in one day and they came in the evening to a wood, where they agreed to spend the night. The donkey and the dog laid themselves down under a great tree, but the cat and the cock went higher—the cock flying up to the topmost branch, where he was safest. Before he went to sleep he looked round towards all the four points of the compass, and he thought he saw a spark shining in the distance. He called to his companions that there must be a house not far off, for he could see a light.

The donkey said, "Then we must rise and go to it, for the lodgings here are very bad"; and the dog said, "Yes; a few bones with a little flesh on them would do me good."

So they took the road in the direction where the light was, till they came to a brilliantly illuminated robbers' house. The donkey, being the biggest, got up at the window and looked in.

"What do you see, Greybeard?" said the cock.

"What do I see?" answered the donkey: "A table covered with beautiful food and drink, and robbers are sitting round it and enjoying themselves."

"That would do nicely for us," said the cock.

"Yes, indeed, if we were only there," replied the donkey.

The animals then consulted together how they should manage to drive out the robbers, till at last they settled on a plan.

The donkey was to place himself with his forefeet on the window-sill, the dog to climb on the donkey's back, and the cat on the dog's, and, lastly, the cock was to fly up and perch himself on the cat's head.

When that was done, at a signal they began their music all together. The donkey brayed, the dog barked, the cat mewed, and the cock crowed; then, with one great smash, they dashed through the window into the room, so that the glass clattered down.

The robbers jumped up at this dreadful noise,

thinking that nothing less than a ghost was coming in, and ran away into the wood in a great fright.

The four companions then sat down at the table, quite content with what was left there, and ate as if they were expecting to fast for a month to come.

When the four musicians had finished they put out the light, and each looked out for a suitable and comfortable sleeping-place.

The donkey lay down in the shed, the dog behind the door, the cat on the hearth near the warm ashes, and the cock set himself on the hen-roost; and as they were all tired with their long journey, they soon went to sleep.

Shortly after midnight, as the robbers in the distance could see that no more lights were burning in the house, and as all seemed quiet, the captain said, "We ought not to have let ourselves be scared so easily," and sent one of them to examine the house.

The messenger found everything quiet, went into the kitchen to light a candle, and thinking the cat's shining fiery eyes were live coals, he held a match to them to light it. But the cat did not understand the joke, flew in his face, spat at him, and scratched. He was dreadfully frightened, ran away, and was going out of the back door, when the dog, who was lying there, jumped up and bit him in the leg. As he ran through the yard, past the shed, the donkey gave him a good kick with his hind foot; and the cock being awakened, and made quite lively by the noise, called out from the hen-roost. "Cock-a-doodle-doo!"

The robber ran as hard as he could back to the captain and cried, "In the house sits a horrid old witch, who flew at me, and scratched my face with her long fingers; and by the door stands a man with a knife, who stabbed me in the leg; and in the shed lies a black monster, who hit me with a club; and up on the roof there sits the judge, who called out, 'Catch the thief, Oh, Do!' So I made the best of my way off."

From that time the robbers never trusted themselves again in the house; but the four musicians liked it so well that they could not make up their minds to leave it, and there spent the remainder of their days.

THE LAMBIKIN

Once upon a time there was a wee wee Lambikin, who frolicked about on his little tottery legs, and enjoyed himself amazingly. Now one day he set off to visit his Granny, and was jumping with joy to think of all the good things he should get from her,

when who should he meet but a Jackal, who looked at
the tender young morsel and said: "Lambikin! Lambikin! I'll EAT YOU!"

But Lambikin only gave a little frisk, and said:

"To Granny's house I go,

Where I shall fatter grow,

Then you can eat me so."

The Jackal thought this reasonable, and let Lambikin pass.

By and by he met a Vulture, and the Vulture, looking hungrily at the tender morsel before him, said: "Lambikin! Lambikin! I'll EAT YOU!"

But Lambikin only gave a little frisk, and said:

"To Granny's house I go,

Where I shall fatter grow,

Then you can eat me so."

The Vulture thought this reasonable, and let Lambikin pass.

And by and by he met a Tiger, and then a Wolf, and a Dog, and an Eagle; and all these, when they saw the tender little morsel said: "Lambikin! Lambikin! I'll EAT YOU!"

But to all of them Lambikin replied:

"To Granny's house I go,

Where I shall fatter grow,

Then you can eat me so."

At last he reached his Granny's house, and said, all in a great hurry: "Granny dear, I've promised to get very fat; so, as people ought to keep their promises, please put me into the corn-bin at once."

So his Granny said he was a good boy, and put him into the corn-bin, and there the greedy little Lambikin stayed for seven days, and ate, and ate, and ate, until he could scarcely waddle, and his Granny said he was fat enough for anything, and must go home.

But cunning little Lambikin said that would never do, for some animal would be sure to eat him on the way back, he was so plump and tender.

"I'll tell you what you must do," said Master Lambikin; "you must make a little drumikin out of the skin of my little brother who died, and then I can sit inside and trundle along nicely, for I'm as tight as a drum myself."

So his Granny made a nice little drumikin out of
his brother's skin, with the wool inside, and Lambikin
curled himself up snug and warm in the middle, and
trundled away gayly. Soon he met with the Eagle,
who called out:

"Drumikin! Drumikin!

Have you seen Lambikin?"

And Mr. Lambikin, curled up in his soft warm nest, replied:

"Fallen into the fire, and so will you.

On little Drumikin! Tum-pa, tum-too!"

"How very annoying!" sighed the Eagle, thinking regretfully of the tender morsel he had let slip.

Meanwhile Lambikin trundled along, laughing to himself, and singing:

"Tum-pa, tum-too;

Tum-pa, tum-too!"

Every animal and bird he met asked him the same question:

"Drumikin! Drumikin!

Have you seen Lambikin?"

And to each of them the little slyboots replied:

"Fallen into the fire, and so will you.

On little Drumikin! Tum-pa, tum-too;

Tum-pa, tum-too; Tum-pa, tum-too!"

Then they all sighed to think of the tender little morsel they had let slip.

At last the Jackal came limping along, for all his sorry looks as sharp as a needle, and he too called out:

"Drumikin! Drumikin!

Have you seen Lambikin?"

And Lambikin, curled up in his snug little nest, replied gayly:

"Fallen into the fire, and so will you.

On little Drumikin! Tum-pa—"

But he never got any farther, for the Jackal recognized his voice at once, and cried: "Hullo! you've turned yourself inside out, have you? Just you come out of that!"

Whereupon he tore open Drumikin and gobbled up Lambikin.

THE THREE BILLY GOATS GRUFF

Once on a time there were three Billy-goats, who
were to go up to the hill-side to make themselves fat, and the name of all three was Gruff.

On the way up was a bridge over a burn they had
to cross; and under the bridge lived a great ugly Troll,

with eyes as big as saucers, and a nose as long as a poker.

So first of all came the youngest billy-goat Gruff to cross the bridge.

"Trip, trap; trip, trap!" went the bridge.

"WHO'S THAT tripping over my bridge?" roared the Troll.

"Oh! it is only I, the tiniest billy-goat Gruff; and I'm going up to the hill-side to make myself fat," said the billy-goat with such a small voice.

"Now, I'm coming to gobble you up," said the Troll.

"Oh, no! pray don't take me. I'm too little, that I

am," said the billy-goat; "wait a bit till the second billy-goat Gruff comes. He's much bigger."

"Well! be off with you," said the Troll.

A little while after came the second billy-goat Gruff to cross the bridge.

"TRIP, TRAP! TRIP, TRAP! TRIP, TRAP!" went the bridge.

"WHO'S THAT tripping over my bridge?" roared the Troll.

"Oh! it's the second billy-goat Gruff, and I'm going up to the hill-side to make myself fat," said the billy-goat, who hadn't such a small voice.

"Now, I'm coming to gobble you up," said the Troll.

"Oh, no! don't take me. Wait a little till the big

billy-goat Gruff comes. He's much bigger."

"Very well! be off with you," said the Troll.

But just then up came the big billy-goat Gruff.

"TRIP, TRAP! TRIP, TRAP! TRIP, TRAP!" went the bridge, for the billy-goat was so heavy that the

bridge creaked and groaned under him.

"WHO'S THAT tramping over my bridge?" roared the Troll.

"IT'S I! THE BIG BILLY-GOAT GRUFF," said the billy-goat, who had an ugly, hoarse voice of his own.

"Now, I'm coming to gobble you up," roared the Troll.

"Well, come along! I've got two spears,
And I'll poke your nose and pierce your ears;
I've got besides two curling-stones,
And I'll bruise your body and rattle your bones."

That was what the big billy-goat said; and so he flew at the Troll, and tossed him out into the burn,

and after that he went up to the hill-side. There the billy-goats got so fat they were scarcely able to walk home again; and if the fat hasn't fallen off them, why they're still fat; and so:

> Snip, snap, snout,
> This tale's told out.

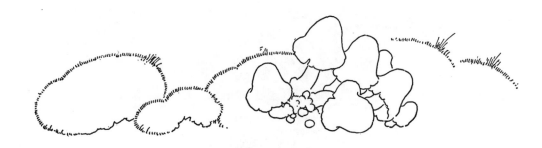

LITTLE TUPPENS

Long, long ago an old hen and her one little chicken went into the woods. The little chicken was named Tuppens. Scratch, scratch, they were busy all day among the leaves finding seeds to eat.

"Do not eat the big seeds," said the old hen to

Little Tuppens, "for they will make you cough."

But by and by Little Tuppens found a big seed and ate it. Then Little Tuppens began to cough. The old hen was frightened at this and ran to the spring.

She said:

"Please, spring, give me some water,
  Little Tuppens is coughing."
The spring said:
  "Get me a cup and then I will
      give you some water."
The old hen ran to the oak-tree and said:
  "Please, oak-tree, give me a cup;
    Then the spring will give me some water.
    Little Tuppens is coughing."
The oak-tree said:
  "Shake me. Then I will give you a cup."
The old hen ran to the little boy and said:
  "Please, little boy, shake the oak-tree;
    Then the oak-tree will give me a cup;

And the spring will give me some water.
Little Tuppens is coughing."
The little boy said:
"Give me some shoes. Then I can shake
the oak-tree for you."

The old hen ran to the shoe-maker and said:

"Please, good shoe-maker, give me

some shoes for the little boy;

Then the little boy will shake the oak-tree;

And the oak-tree will give me a cup;

And the spring will give me some water.

Little Tuppens is coughing."

The shoe-maker said:

"Get me some leather and then I will make

some shoes for the little boy."

The old hen ran to the cow and said:

"Please, cow, give me some leather;

Then the shoe-maker will make

shoes for the little boy;

And the little boy will shake the oak-tree;

And the oak-tree will give me a cup;

And the spring will give me some water.

Little Tuppens is coughing."

The cow said:

"Get me some corn and then I will

give you some leather."

The old hen ran to the farmer and said:

"Please, farmer, give me corn for the cow;
  Then the cow will give me some leather
    for the shoe-maker;
  And the shoe-maker will make shoes
    for the little boy;

And the little boy will shake the oak-tree;

And the oak-tree will give me a cup;

And the spring will give me some water.

Little Tuppens is coughing.''

The farmer said:

"Get me a plow and then I can
give you some corn."
The old hen ran to the blacksmith and said:
"Please, good blacksmith, give me
a plow for the farmer;

Then the farmer will give me some
   corn for the cow;
And the cow will give me some
   leather for the shoe-maker;
And the shoe-maker will give me
   some shoes for the little boy;
And the little boy will shake the oak-tree;
And the oak-tree will give me a cup;
And the spring will give me some water;
Little Tuppens is coughing.
The blacksmith said:
  "Get me some iron and then I can
    give you a plow."
The old hen ran to the dwarfs and asked for some iron for the blacksmith.

When she had told her story about Little Tuppens to the dwarfs, they wanted to help. They went into their cave and brought out some iron for the blacksmith.

Then the blacksmith made a plow
   for the farmer;
And the farmer gave some corn for the cow;

And the cow gave some leather
    for the shoe-maker;
And the shoe-maker made some shoes
    for the little boy;
And the little boy shook the oak-tree;

And the oak-tree gave a cup;

And the spring gave some water;

And the old hen gave the water
   to Little Tuppens

And Little Tuppens stopped coughing.

THE WOLF and THE FOX

A wolf, once upon a time, caught a fox. It happened one day that they were both going through the forest, and the wolf said to his companion: "Get me some food, or I will eat you up."

The fox replied: "I know a farmyard where there

are a couple of young lambs, which, if you wish, we
will fetch.''

This proposal pleased the wolf, so they went, and
the fox, stealing first one of the lambs, brought it to
the wolf, and then ran away. The wolf devoured it

quickly, but was not contented and went to fetch the other lamb by himself, but he did it so awkwardly that he aroused the attention of the mother, who began to cry and bleat loudly, so that the peasants ran up.

There they found the wolf, and beat him so unmercifully that he ran, howling and limping, to the fox, and said: "You have led me to a nice place, for, when I went to fetch the other lamb, the peasants came and beat me terribly!"

"Why are you such a glutton?" asked the fox.

The next day they went again into the fields.

The covetous wolf said to the fox: "Get me something to eat now, or I will devour you!"

The fox said he knew a country house where the cook was going that evening to make some pancakes, and thither they went. When they arrived, the fox sneaked and crept around the house until he at last discovered where the dish was standing, out of which he stole six pancakes, and took them to the wolf. "There is something for you to eat!" said the fox and then ran away.

The wolf dispatched these in a minute or two, and, wishing to taste some more, he went and seized the dish, but took it away so hurriedly that it broke in pieces. The noise of its fall brought out the woman. As soon as she saw the wolf, the woman called her people, who, hastening up, beat him with such a good will that he ran home to the fox, howling, with two lame legs!

"What a horrid place you have drawn me into now," cried he; "the peasants have caught me, and dressed my skin finely!"

"Why, then, are you such a glutton?" said the fox.

When they went out again the third day, the wolf limping along with weariness, he said to the fox: "Get me something to eat now, or I will devour you!"

The fox said he knew a man who had just killed a pig, and salted the meat down in a cask in his cellar, and that they could get at it. The wolf replied that he would go with him on condition that he helped him if

he could not escape. "Oh, of course I will, on mine own account!" said the fox, and showed him the tricks and ways by which they could get into the cellar. When they went in there was meat in abundance, and the wolf was enraptured at the sight. The fox, too, had a taste, but kept looking around while eating, and ran frequently to the hole by which they had entered, to see if his body would slip through it easily.

Presently the wolf asked: "Why are you running about so, you fox, jumping in and out?" "I want to see if any one is coming," replied the fox cunningly; "but mind you do not eat too much!"

The wolf said he would not leave till the cask was quite empty; and meanwhile the peasant, who had heard the noise made by the fox, entered the cellar. The fox, as soon as he saw him, made a spring, and was through the hole in a jiffy; and the wolf tried to follow his example, but he had eaten so much that his body was too big for the opening, and he stuck fast.

Then came the peasants with cudgels, and beat him sorely; but the fox leaped away into the forest, very glad to get rid of the old glutton.

THE CAT and the MOUSE

The cat and the mouse
  Play'd in the malt-house:
 · The cat bit the mouse's tail off. "Pray, puss, give
me my tail."

"No," says the cat, "I'll not give you your tail till

you go to the cow and fetch me some milk."

First she leapt, and then she ran,

Till she came to the cow, and thus began:

"Pray, Cow, give me milk, that I may give cat milk, that cat may give me my tail again."

"No," said the cow, "I will give you no milk till
you go to the farmer and get me some hay."
First she leapt, and then she ran,
Till she came to the farmer, and thus began:
"Pray, Farmer, give me hay, that I may give cow

hay, that cow may give me milk, that I may give cat milk, that cat may give me my own tail again."

"No," says the farmer, "I'll give you no hay till you go to the butcher and fetch me some meat."

First she leapt, and then she ran,

Till she came to the butcher, and thus began:

"Pray, Butcher, give me meat, that I may give farmer meat, that farmer may give me hay, that I may give cow hay, that cow may give me milk, that I may give cat milk, that cat may give me my own tail again."

"No," says the butcher, "I'll give you no meat till you go to the baker and fetch me some bread."

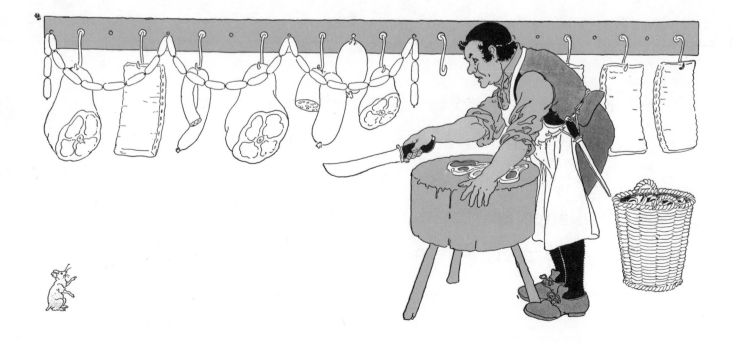

First she leapt, and then she ran,

Till she came to the baker, and thus began:

"Pray, Baker, give me bread, that I may give butcher bread, that butcher may give me meat, that I may give farmer meat, that farmer may give me hay, that I may give cow hay, that cow may give me milk, that I may give cat milk, that cat may give me my own tail again."

"Yes," says the baker, "I'll give you bread,

But if you eat my meal, I'll cut off your head."

Then the baker gave mouse bread, and mouse gave butcher bread, and butcher gave mouse meat, and mouse gave farmer meat, and farmer gave mouse hay, and mouse gave cow hay, and cow gave mouse milk, and mouse gave cat milk, and cat gave mouse her own tail again.

The HOUSE ON THE HILL

Once upon a time a curly-tailed pig said to his
friend the sheep, "I am tired of living in a
pen. I am going to build me a house on the hill."

"Oh! may I go with you?" said the sheep.

"What can you do to help?" asked the pig.

"I can haul the logs for the house," said the sheep.

"Good!" said the pig. "You are just the one I want.
You may go with me."

As the pig and the sheep walked and talked about
their new house, they met a goose.

"Good morning, pig," said the goose. "Where are
you going this fine morning?"

"We are going to the hill to build us a house. I am
tired of living in a pen," said the pig.

"Quack!" said the goose. "May I go with you?"

"What can you do to help?" asked the pig.

"I can gather moss, and stuff it into the cracks to keep out the rain."

"Good!" said the pig and the sheep. "You are just the one we want. You may go with us."

As the pig and the sheep and the goose walked and talked about their new house, they met a rabbit.

"Good morning, rabbit," said the pig.

"Good morning," said the rabbit. "Where are you going this fine morning?"

"We are going to the hill to build us a house. I am tired of living in a pen," said the pig.

"Oh!" said the rabbit, with a quick little jump. "May I go with you?"

"What can you do to help?" asked the pig.

"I can dig holes for the posts of your house," said
the rabbit.

"Good!" said the pig and the sheep and the goose.
"You are just the one we want. You may go with us."

As the pig and the sheep and the goose and the rabbit walked and talked about their new house, they met a cock.

"Good morning, cock," said the pig.

"Good morning," said the cock. "Where are you

going this fine morning?"

"We are going to build us a house. I am tired of living in a pen," said the pig.

The cock flapped his wings three times. "Oh, Oh, Oh, O-O-Oh!" he crowed. "May I go with you?"

"What can you do to help?" asked the pig.

"I can be your clock," said the cock. "I will crow every morning and waken you at daybreak."

"Good!" said the pig and the sheep and the goose and the rabbit. "You are just the one we want. You may go with us."

Then they all went happily to the hill. The pig found the logs for the house. The sheep hauled them together. The rabbit dug the holes for the posts. The

goose stuffed moss in the cracks to keep out the rain. And every morning the cock crowed to waken the workers. When at last the house was finished, the cock flew to the very top of it, and crowed and crowed and crowed.